The Kids'
Library of
Personal Safety

A Kid's Guide
to Staying Safe at
SCHOOL

Maribeth Boelts

The Rosen Publishing Group's
PowerKids Press™
New York

Published in 1997 by The Rosen Publishing Group, Inc.
29 East 21st Street, New York, NY 10010

First Edition

Book Design: Erin McKenna

Photo Credits: Cover and all photographs by Carrie Ann Grippo.

Boelts, Maribeth, 1964–
      A kid's guide to staying safe at school /by Maribeth Boelts.
          p.   cm. — (The kids' library of personal safety)
      Includes index.
      Summary: Explains school safety, including tips on how to stay safe on the school bus, what to do about peer pressure and violence, and what to do about weapons at school.
      ISBN 0-8239-5079-4 (lib. bdg.)
      1. Schools—Safety measures—Juvenile literature. 2. Safety education—Juvenile literature. [1. Schools—Safety measures. 2. Safety.] I. Title. II. Series.
      LB2864.5.B64 1997
      363.11'9371—dc21
                                                                                  96-30001
                                                                                       CIP
                                                                                        AC

Manufactured in the United States of America

Contents

John and Justin

John raced down the stairs. He was excited. It was the first time his parents were going to let him walk to school without them.

"John, remember what we talked about," his dad said.

"I know, Dad. I remember everything about staying safe," John said. John's friend, Justin, knocked on the door.

"Let's go, John," Justin said. "I'm glad we can walk to school together."

◀ It's fun to be grown-up enough to walk safely to school with your friends.

Walking to School

School is an exciting place. It's where you learn new things and make good friends. School should also be a safe place. You can help make it safe by following the rules that your parents and teachers tell you about.

The first rule for school safety is about getting to school. If you walk to school, your parents can help you choose a safe path to take when you walk. Once you know the way, stick to it. Shortcuts may sound like a good idea, but they can be **dangerous** (DAYN-jer-us).

Be smart: Walk with a buddy or two ▶ when you go to and from school.

School Bus Safety

Many kids travel to school on a school bus. To make sure everyone is safe, there are rules to remember when riding the bus. Always sit down in your seat. Always wear your seat belt. Never stick your hands and arms out the windows. Your teacher and the bus driver will tell you what the other rules are.

The bus driver's job is to make sure that you get to and from school safely. You can help him or her by talking quietly when you're on the bus. Make sure you listen to the bus driver. Safe bus riding is the smart way to go!

Find a seat as soon as you get on the bus.

School Rules

Everyone at school must follow the rules. Even your teacher has to follow the rules!

The most important rule is always to listen to your teacher. Your teacher is there to help you. Some of his or her rules may seem silly or unfair to you, but they are important. They are there so that you and your friends can learn, have fun, and stay safe at school.

Whether you are in the classroom or at the playground, listening to your teacher is very important. ▶

Recess

Most kids love recess. It is a great time to talk to friends and play games. But did you know that there are rules at recess too?

Be sure to share games and playground **equipment** (ee-KWIP-ment) with others. There are **monitors** (MON-ih-terz) or teachers who watch over children at recess. If something happens that is bad or scary, tell the teacher or monitor. They are there to help you.

If you see a stranger at recess, tell your teacher or monitor right away.

◀ Rules at recess may not be fun, but they help everyone to stay safe.

13

Saying No

Staying safe at school also means being smart about choosing friends. True friends don't **pressure** (PREH-sher) each other to do unsafe things, such as take drugs, get into fights, or break school rules.

If someone does pressure you to do something that you think is wrong, the best thing to do is say "No." Walk away and tell a grown-up. It takes **courage** (KUR-ej) to make good decisions and do what is right. But making good decisions helps keep you safe.

14

It might be scary if someone asks you to do something you don't wan't to do, but you can say no and then tell a grown-up. ▶

Violence Doesn't Help

Arguments (AR-gyoo-mentz) can happen during recess or in the classroom. Using **violence** (VY-uh-lentz), such as hitting, kicking, or pushing to try to fix an argument is dangerous. It can actually make the problem worse. And violence is against school rules.

There is a better and safer way to solve an argument or a problem with your friends. You can tell the other person how you feel. Then you can talk about it together.

◀ The best way to work out an argument between you and a friend is to talk about it together.

Talk It Out

It can be hard to talk about how you feel when you are angry or when your feelings are hurt. But you can do it. Here are some things you might say to someone when you are having a disagreement:

"I don't like being pushed. Please stop."

"It's my jump rope, but I don't mind if we take turns using it."

If you need help, your teacher, **counselor** (KOWN-sih-ler), or principal can **mediate** (MEE-dee-ayt). That means they will listen to both sides of the argument and help you both decide what to do next.

A mediator will give both people in an argument a chance to say how they feel. ▶

No Place for Weapons

Some kids think that they will be safer at school if they carry a **weapon** (WEP-un). They might bring a knife or even a gun to school. Bringing any type of weapon to school is against the rules and against the law. It's also very dangerous. You could wind up hurting yourself or someone else. If you know someone at school who has a weapon, be sure to tell your teacher, counselor, or principal right away.

◀ Carrying a weapon doesn't make you tougher. It only makes things worse.

A Favorite Place

School is a place to learn new things and make good friends. It's a place where you should feel safe and ready to find out more about the world. The grown-ups at school are there because they want to help you to learn and grow. You can talk to them if you ever have a problem or feel unsafe.

By following the school rules, choosing true friends, and working hard, school can be one of your favorite places!

Glossary

argument (AR-gyoo-ment) When people disagree.

counselor (KOWN-sih-ler) A grown-up at school who is trained to help kids with their worries or problems.

courage (KUR-ej) Being brave.

dangerous (DAYN-jer-us) Something that is unsafe or harmful.

equipment (ee-KWIP-ment) Things to play on in a park or playground.

mediate (MEE-dee-ayt) To listen to both sides of an argument and then decide how to solve it.

monitor (MON-ih-ter) A grown-up whose job is to watch kids at recess and to help if anything happens.

pressure (PREH-sher) To make someone feel like they have to do something.

violence (VY-uh-lentz) To cause injury or damage.

weapon (WEP-un) An object that can do harm to someone else.

Index

24